THE KEEPER OF THE GATE

Three Lovecraftian Stories

William Meikle

CONTENTS

THE KEEPER OF THE GATE

We almost went off the road twice, lights flashing and sirens blaring, doing forty on the bends despite the snow. *Shots fired* was the message.

We were too late to stop any bullets hitting their targets—and far too late to catch the shooter. Two bodies—two children—lay in the driveway, half-naked and already freezing, single gunshot wounds to the back of the head. The father sat in the hall just inside the door—shot in the left eye with an exit wound that had taken off the back of his skull and decorated the wall in Jackson Pollock red.

"Where's the mother?" Jake Rogers asked me, but I didn't have an answer.

We searched the house and did a tour around the outside. Ours were the only footprints in the snow, and there were none around the dead girls' bodies. No tire tracks either.

"Did the father do it, then do himself?" Jake asked.

"If so, where's the weapon?" I replied.

That had us both stumped.

We had a wait ahead of us—the forensics boys were tied up on another shooting downtown—Saturday night in the city this close to Christmas brought out more crazies than normal, and tonight was no exception. Jake and I were used to seeing shooting victims—just not out here in the 'burbs on the coast, and not pre-teen girls lying half-naked in snowy driveways. I'll admit I was more than a bit twitchy as we stood in the relative warmth of the hallway waiting for the cavalry to show up.

Matters didn't improve any when the chanting started up in the cellar.

"Didn't you check down there?" I whispered.

Jake had his gun out already.

"I thought you did."

The chanting got louder—there were at least three voices, maybe more.

Jake reached for the door handle. As soon as his fingers touched it the chanting stopped, like a needle taken off a vinyl record. Everything went quiet again.

"Cover me," Jake whispered, and pulled the door open.

There seemed to be nothing but darkness beyond, but Jake wasn't to be deterred. I followed him, gingerly, down the cellar steps.

"Armed police," he shouted. "We're coming down. Don't do anything stupid."

There was no response. I got my flashlight off my belt and switched it on, the sudden flare of light almost blinding me so that at first all I could see was the back of Jake's head.

There was still no sound from below, and the place was so quiet and dark I started to wonder whether we'd actually heard what we thought we'd heard. Then there was a shuffling scrape, as of something heavy being dragged across a dirt floor.

"Don't move," Jake shouted.

I swung the flashlight down, but with Jake in the way, the space was too confined to show me anything beyond a couple of square yards at the foot of the steps.

There was another scrape, deeper in the darkness. Somebody moaned—a woman, in some pain.

The mother?

"Armed police," Jake shouted again. If I didn't know him so well I might not have noticed the tremor in his voice. "Come on out where we can see you."

Jake stepped off the steps onto the cellar floor, giving me space to move the beam of the flashlight around. I saw the pale shape in the gloom just before lighting up the body. She lay spread-eagled, naked on a circular diagram that had been crudely scratched in the dirt. Whoever had moaned, it hadn't been her—her dead eyes stared at the ceiling although there was no obvious sign of any wound. A gun lay on the floor, just outside the etched circle.

Jake dropped into a crouch and pointed his own weapon into the far-left corner.

"I see you, back there," he shouted. "Come on out."

I swung the light around to where Jake was aiming, but all I found were rough walls and storage crates.

"What did you see, Jake?"

He didn't reply. I swung the light around to look him in the eye. He was as white as a sheet, and shaking. He turned on his heels and went back up the steps, almost running.

I stood there for long seconds, turning in a full circle, searching the whole space. I was quite alone in the cellar.

The father's prints were the only ones on the gun. The case was closed almost before we finished the paperwork. Neither the chanting nor the moaning made their way into our reports—Jake and I both knew that would just lead to questions we couldn't answer. *Murder, suicide* was the verdict and it was all tied up in a pretty bow for public consumption. I wasn't happy, but I couldn't see what else could be done.

Jake had other ideas.

I found him in his usual perch at O'Hara's—far end of the bar near the Guinness tap. He had a pint of the black stuff waiting for me.

"Did the Captain tell you how the father shot himself then threw the gun down into the cellar?" he asked. He sounded weary, but there was something else there too, something I couldn't quite identify. "Did he tell you how the wife died of shock on finding him and fell down the stairs, just happening to land dead center on that...whatever it was? And all of this through a closed cellar door?"

"I don't think they want anyone to look too closely, Jake," I replied. "They don't want a scandal. The father was some kind of big cheese in finance. You know what happens in those cases—ranks get closed, favors get called in..."

"...and questions get quietly buried. Yeah. I know."

"That's not what's eating you, is it?" I asked. "We've played the game too often for this one to be getting to you."

He ordered two whiskeys—that's when I knew it was serious.

"I saw something," he said softly. "Down in that cellar. I saw something."

I knew now what I was seeing in his eyes—it was fear, and that got me scared, for big Jake Rogers had never been afraid of anything in his life.

I downed my whiskey in one.

"Tell me," I said.

At first I wasn't sure I was going to get an answer, and when I did it was in a managed whisper so that only I would hear.

"It was just dim lights at first," he said. "A dancing pattern of lights. I thought it might be her ghost."

If anyone else had said that to me, I'd have laughed it off, but Jake wasn't a man prone to flights of fancy. Work, booze and football were his holy trinity; for him, fiction was something read by people who couldn't handle reality.

"What do you mean?" I asked, not entirely sure I wanted to know.

"I only caught a glimpse—you know that, you were there. It was only a dark shadow when I first glanced at it. I thought it was a woman, hunched over, standing deep in the corner. But just before you shone the light over that way, I got a good look. You know those pictures the telescope in space takes—galaxies and nebulas and gas clouds and shit? Like that—only small, in the corner, but big at the same time, as if I could have walked into it —walked into infinity and never looked back."

He'd got it all out fast, as if afraid to stop. Now I didn't know what to say in reply.

"Jake, we'd just had a shock and..."

"I know what I saw," he said, interrupting me. "This isn't over. Something happened in that house. That family were murdered—all of them. I'm going to find out who did it."

What can I say? Jake had been my partner for more than a decade. The next day, we started digging.

We had to keep it off the books, so it was slow going at first, snatching what time we could to look into the families' life. The father, John Mitchell, was a bigwig in a trading house—he managed futures in commodities, effectively guessing which way the market might go, and backing his best guesses with cash—lots of cash. There was motive aplenty in that cash—the kind of amounts that attracts shysters like flies to shit.

But this didn't smell like a robbery gone bad—it was messy, but not messy enough.

We went deeper. Jake got Mitchell's laptop from

evidence—don't ask—and we had Joe Kaspervitch go through it for us. Our fifty bucks didn't get us much, but it got us Mitchell's last draft email—one he never got round to sending, and one that started Jake's gears grinding in the right direction.

"I want out," it read. "It's getting too close now. The risk isn't worth the reward. We should stop while we're ahead."

Unfortunately there was no sign of any intended recipients, but Jake had a sniff of conspiracy in his nose now.

We dug deeper still.

We discovered that Mitchell was just one of a group of businessmen—rising stars if you like—who, in the last eighteen months, had taken the sector by storm, making money hand over fist in the Futures markets like no one had ever managed before. There was talk of methods, patterns, even a faint whiff of skullduggery, but the bottom line was that these guys were getting rich fast, and no one knew how they were doing it.

"We should talk to these other guys," Jake said, We were back in O'Hara's, on the black stuff. The case had its hooks in my partner now, and like a terrier with a bone, he was in no mood to let go. "Look at that last email again. Mitchell wanted out—that would threaten the gravy train. There's our motive, right there."

"We can't," I said, trying to be the voice of reason. "The case is closed, and so are the ranks of the great and good. We can't go charging around like a bull in a china shop—we've got no evidence."

Jake smiled and I realized I'd fallen into his trap.

"Well, let's go find some then. There must be something in the Mitchell house that everybody missed."

Disturbing a crime scene was enough to get us both shit-canned, but I didn't mention it as we opened the door, slipped under the tape and went into the dark hallway—it wasn't as if this was our first time at this particular dance.

For half an hour I thought Jake was going to be disappointed. We went through the ground floor fast—nothing to see but the normal domestic habits of a family with two kids—and a stain on the hallway wall I didn't like to look at too closely.

Upstairs proved little more fruitful, although a search of the study delivered a small notebook tucked in the back of a drawer that contained columns of letters and figures that were obviously in some sort of code. Jake pocketed that, and finally we headed to the one place neither of us really wanted to go—down into the dark cellar.

Despite our best efforts, neither of us could find a light switch, so we both had our flashlights lit as we went down—me first this time. My fingers were twitching to draw my weapon—it felt like the situation demanded it, but I knew it was just my mind reminding me of the last time. Even so, I half expected to see a naked corpse on the dusty floor when I reached the foot of the steps. I let out a sigh of relief when a sweep of the torch showed nothing but the etched circle of strange pictograms, the design partially scuffed and smudged by the footprints of the cops and forensics men that had come through here.

A bulb burst into light just above my head, almost blinding me. I turned to see Jake, hand on a switch.

"Well, that's something at least," he replied, and smiled, although I saw the same tension in his eyes that I felt in my chest.

We made a search of the room, each of us—consciously or otherwise, working around the drawn marks on the floor, as if fearful of stepping on—or worse, inside, the lines. There was nothing to see but packing cases, packed earth and dry walls. I was about to admit defeat when Jake hushed me into silence.

"Do you hear it?" he whispered.

If I hadn't known Jake better, I might have thought he was about to take a powder. Then I heard it too—distant chanting, getting louder.

"Where the fuck is it coming from?" I whispered, suddenly afraid to raise my voice. The chanting got closer—a strange, guttural cacophony that contained no words of any language I could recognize. At that point I wasn't even sure that human vocal chords were capable of making the sounds we heard—yips and cries, chirps and whistles intermingled with bass drones and harsh glottal stops. The whole effect chilled me to the bone, exaggerated by a sudden blast of cold air that swept through the room like a gale.

"Somebody opened a window," I said.

"I don't think so," Jake replied, and pointed into the left-hand corner of the room.

At first it was just a darker shadow that seemed to suck the light away, leaving only bitter cold behind. My eyes strained to make out detail as the chanting rang in my ears and the room vibrated in sympathy. The light fitting swung lazily in time.

My whole body shook, vibrating with the rhythm. My head swam, and it seemed as if the walls of the cellar melted and ran. The light receded into a great distance until it was little more than a pinpoint in a blanket of darkness, and I was alone, in a cathedral of emptiness where nothing existed save the dark and the pounding chant.

I saw stars—vast swathes of gold and blue and silver, all dancing in great purple and red clouds that spun webs of grandeur across unending vistas. Shapes moved in and among the nebulae; dark, wispy shadows casting a pallor over whole galaxies at a time, shadows that capered and whirled as the dance grew ever more frenetic. I was buffeted, as if by a strong, surging tide, but as the beat grew ever stronger I cared little. I gave myself to it, lost in the dance, lost in the stars.

I don't know how long I wandered in the space between. I forgot myself, forgot Jake, dancing in the vastness where only rhythm mattered.

After a while I dreamed. I dreamed a funeral—an open coffin where Jake's pale face stared up at me, a face I could barely see through my tears. I stretched out a hand to touch his cheek.

A gunshot brought me back—reeled in like a hooked fish, tugged reluctantly through a too tight opening and emerging into the blazing light of a cold cellar.

Jake stood in a firing crouch, emptying a clip into the corner. I drew my own gun and joined in, despite not being able to see anything but darker shadow. My ears rang, almost deafened by the shots in the close confinement. All too quickly my trigger pulled on empty. The echoes died away leaving dead silence behind.

Jake and I stood in a quiet, empty cellar that suddenly felt warm and stifling. We took one look at each other and headed for the steps at a run. He beat me to it, just, but I was level by the time we barrelled through the hallway and stumbled, almost fell, out into the driveway. A blanket of cold stars mocked us from on high as we drove off, leaving a squeal of tires in our wake.

"What the fuck just happened?"

O'Hara's bar again, and more of the black stuff, helped down with whiskey. Jake hadn't spoken since we left the cellar, but at least his hands stopped shaking as we headed into the second pint of Guinness.

"Magician's tricks and fucking hocus-pocus," he said. "That's what fucking happened. I told you there was something hinky going on. I fucking told you."

What I'd seen—and felt—back in the cellar was a bit more than *hinky*, but I knew when to keep my mouth shut if nothing else.

"We're onto something," Jake said. "Somebody just tried to warn us off."

"Actually, I think they succeeded," I said, and got more of the Guinness inside me, trying to make a warm spot in a body that still held too much memory of dancing a cold empty vastness.

Jake took out the small notebook—I'd forgotten all about it, but he'd had it in his pocket the whole time.

"This is it," he said. "This is the thing that will crack the case open for us."

I wasn't sure where he was getting his certainty, but I trusted his instincts. He started to rifle through the pages.

"Maybe we should just leave it alone?" I said. "I saw something back there. I..."

"I don't want to know," Jake replied. It wasn't fear in his eyes this time—it was pleading. "Whatever we saw, it was just a trick. What else could it be?"

That was a question I asked myself all the way home. I fell into bed, but sleep was a long time in coming. When I finally drifted off I fell into dreams of dancing galaxies, naked women lying on crudely carved circles and Jake's dead eyes staring up at me through my tears.

I didn't feel rested on wakening, and when I got to work we caught a drive-by shooting that took us most of the morning to wrap up. When we finally got a quiet minute back at the precinct, Jake pulled me aside next to the coffee machine.

"I showed Kaspervitch the notebook. He say's it's a simple substitution cipher. He's working on it now. We should get the gen in an hour or so."

"And then what?" I asked. I was weary. I couldn't see an end on Jake's current path that I liked, and I kept seeing that last dream, of him in the coffin. I started to get a real bad feeling, and what I wanted more than anything else was to just lose myself in the daily grind and forget all about the Mitchell case. But Jake was my partner, and that bought him a lot of slack. I decided to back his play —for the time being at least.

He hadn't noticed my reticence.

"I told you—we'll crack this case wide open. We're

onto something. I feel it in my water."

All I felt in mine was cold, a deep chill that even copious amounts of black coffee wouldn't shift. Jake whispered something as we went back to our desks. I didn't quite catch it, and didn't know how important it would prove.

"I've seen it."

"It's a diary," Kaspervitch said, dropping the notebook on Jake's desk and making Jake's fifty disappear into an inside pocket. "Dates and places, I'm guessing of some kind of business meetings, for a lot of the names in his email contacts turn up in there too. But if they are business meetings, the times and places are off—unless I've made a mistake, all these meetings take place in quiet spots, in the middle of the night."

Jake looked up at me and smiled.

"See—I told you it was hinky."

He turned to Kaspervitch.

"So when's the next one pencilled in?"

"Two days time—but he won't be there, will he?" Kaspervitch said.

"He won't. But we will," Jake replied. He had his game face on and the bit between his teeth. Nothing I could say now was going to make any difference. All I could do was tag along, and hope I could prevent the coffin dream from ever coming to pass.

The Thursday meeting was due for two in the morning in a disused warehouse in the docks. Jake and I got there early, around midnight. We parked well away from the place and walked in through the alleyways of derelict offices and factories. Both our fathers had worked here, way back when, and as kids we'd ran together through these same docks, filled then with workmen and noise and vitality. Now they were as dead as the cellar beneath the Mitchell house, and damned near as cold. We took up a spot in the girders that made up what was left of the rafters of the warehouse, and tried to make ourselves comfortable for what might prove to be a lengthy stake-out.

Jake was quiet, scarily so, for I've rarely met a more voluble man, but he seemed content to sit and watch. He wouldn't allow any discussion of the events in the cellar. I couldn't really blame him for that—but I also couldn't help but wonder whether he had seen a dream of his own—and whether he might have been looking down at me in a coffin in his version.

My butt was starting to get numb from the cold seeping up through the girders when we finally saw some action. We were alerted firstly by the slam of car doors—two followed by a third a minute later. After a delay, three men, dressed in long, hooded robes that might have been comical in another situation, walked into the warehouse from the west-end and immediately started drawing diagrams and circles on the floor. The end result was all too familiar—it seemed to perfectly match the one that had been etched beneath Mrs. Mitchell's dead body.

I realized I was holding my breath, waiting for something—distant chanting maybe, or another vision of the cold depths of space. What I didn't expect was for one of the three figures to stand in the center of the diagram, turn, and look straight up at our position.

"You can come down now," a deep male voice said. "The show's about to begin and you'll get a better view from here."

Jake didn't seem in the slightest surprised by the turn of events, leading me to wonder again what it was that he had seen in our time in the cellar. I was still wondering as we clambered down through a tangle of metal and girders to the floor of the warehouse.

The tall robed man was so polite it was almost surreal.

"Welcome, gentlemen," he said. "We've been expecting you."

"You saw it in advance, didn't you?" Jake said. "That's what you do—you use some kind of new trick to see what's going to happen."

"Oh, it's not a trick, I assure you," the robed man said. "And it's not new either—the Gatekeeper has been showing people the way since time began. You'll see for yourselves soon enough."

"I've got no intention of seeing any more," Jake said. He drew his gun and aimed it directly at the robed figure's chest. The other two—neither of whom had yet said a word, stood several paces further back, but showed no sign of getting involved.

"Jake," I whispered. "We can't do anything here. We've no proof of anything."

Jake waved his pistol towards the tall man.

"He did it—I know he did—he killed the Mitchell family."

The tall man laughed.

"Is that what this is about? I'm afraid you have it all wrong. Mitchell saw what needed doing at our last meeting. His wife was going to die—he saw it, and he knew it—that's the way it works. Once something is seen, it cannot be changed. Poor Mitchell couldn't handle it. He snapped—and you saw the results. And of course, his poor wife died anyway—such a shame."

He didn't sound in the slightest bit concerned, either at the death of Mitchell and his family, or by the fact he had a gun pointed at him.

Jake's earlier calm was rapidly being replaced by anger.

"That's not what happened—there's no way Mitchell could have done it—his gun was in the cellar."

"Oh, I did that," the tall man said casually. "I had to, you see—I saw it, so it had to happen. And I think I'm beginning to understand why it had to happen. It brought you here, to this place, this time. It brought you to the Gate. Yog-Sothoth has something for you to see."

We'd just taken a jump—another one—into the Twilight Zone. This wasn't going the way either of us would have predicted. Or rather, not as I would have predicted, for Jake seemed to know exactly what he was doing. He raised his gun.

The robed man drew a knife from up his left sleeve—a long curved thing with writing carved along the length of the blade.

"Put down your weapon, sir," Jake said.

"I assure you, it's purely ceremonial," he said, and raised it above his head.

"Put down the weapon or I'll shoot."

"You'll do what you have to do," the man said sadly. "I've already seen it."

He lifted the knife high, stepped forward and let out a yell.

"Ia!"

Jake put two bullets in him.

The tall man fell to the ground, grunted twice and coughed up blood all over the chalk circle.

Jake stood over the body, eyes glazed as if he was not really sure what he'd just done. I wasn't sure what to do about it—by rights I should have hauled him off downtown, but he was my partner—I trusted him. I just hoped I was going to be able to believe his reasoning.

As it turned out, I didn't have time to think. A colder chill blew through the warehouse, and behind it came the first distant sounds of chanting.

"Step out of the circle," one of the robed figures said. "Please, step out of the circle."

I took a step back—all that was needed to get me beyond the widest extent of the drawing—but Jake stood his ground, standing over the prone robed body.

The chanting got louder, the same dissonant mixture of singing, yips and screams we'd heard in the cellar.

"Jake—I think you should get out of there."

"Don't worry, pal," he said, grimly. "I know what needs doing—I've seen it."

The cold bit at my bones, and the chanting rose to echo and ring all around the warehouse. Something shifted—I can't describe it any better than that, and that's exactly what if felt like—a shifting to somewhere subtly elsewhere—or elsewhen.

It started small; a tear in the fabric of reality, no bigger than a sliver of fingernail, appeared in the center of the circle above Jake's head and hung there. As I watched it settled into a new configuration, a black oily droplet held quivering in empty air.

The walls of the warehouse throbbed like a heartbeat. The black egg pulsed in time. And now it was more than obvious—it was growing.

It calved, and calved again.

Four eggs hung in a tight group above Jake's head, pulsing in time with the rising cacophony of the chanting. Colors danced and flowed across the sheer black surfaces; blues and greens and shimmering silvers on the eggs.

In the blink of an eye there were eight.

I was vaguely aware of Jake shouting, but I was past caring, lost in contemplation of the beauty before me.

Sixteen now, all perfect, all dancing.

The chanting grew louder still.

Thirty two now, and they had started to fill the warehouse with dancing aurora of shimmering lights that pulsed and capered in time with the throb of magic and the screams of the chant, everything careening along in a big happy dance.

Sixty-four, each a shimmering pearl of black light.

The colors filled the room, spilled out over the circle, crept around my feet, danced in my eyes, in my head, all though my body. I gave myself to it, willingly. The warehouse filled with stars, and we danced among them.

I strained to turn my head towards the eggs.

A hundred and twenty eight now, and already calving

into two hundred and fifty-six.

Jake had tears in his eyes as he looked at me.

"This is how it has to be," he said.

The protective circle enfolded what I guessed to be a thousand and twenty four eggs. Jake lifted his gun and emptied the clip into them.

Several things happened at once. The myriad of bubbles popped, burst and disappeared as if they had never been there at all. Jake screamed—a wail that in itself was enough to set the walls throbbing and quaking. Swirling clouds seem to come from nowhere to fill the room with darkness. Everything went black as a pit of hell, and a thunderous blast rocked the warehouse, driving me down into a place where I dreamed of empty spaces filled with oily, glistening bubbles. They popped and spawned yet more bubbles, then even more, until I swam in a swirling sea of colors.

I drifted.

When I got back—was given back—to what passes for reality, thin daylight lit the floor of the warehouse. There was no sign of the two robed figures—nor of the body of the man that Jake had shot. The chalk circle on the floor, and any blood that had been there, had been scuffed and scraped into the dust so much that any forensics gathering would be almost impossible.

Jake lay on his back, dead eyes staring up at me.

I didn't shed a tear in the warehouse, but the funeral is later today. I have to do my best not to cry, but I fear that I will.

This is how it has to be.

OUT OF THE BLACK

Ten short years.

That's how long we have. The ore that gives us light, keeps us warm, and runs the food plants has finally come to an end. Three hundred and fifty years after the dimming. A good run.

But not long enough. Not by my reckoning. I'm only twelve points short of my breeding merit. There's no way I'm checking out of here before then.

So I volunteered. "Exploration duty", that's what they call it. "Suicide", Tom Draper said. "Escape", Linda whispered in my ear the night before I left.

As it turns out, all three were right in their own way.

It started well enough, despite my apprehension at

heading out. The flyer they gave me hadn't been upside for thirty years; nobody had. Too cold, too dark, no point. Until now. I had to wait for two days while the bots fitted an ore probe and a drill and that just gave me more time to fret. I was actually happy when I strapped in and took the flyer into the tube.

The five-minute ascent to Hell soon put paid to that.

I felt cold before we got halfway up. Of course I knew about Hell. No light for three hundred years, thirty foot thick ice shelves and no life bigger than a patch of lichen. I *knew* that. I just didn't realise what it meant in real terms.

At least the flyer had a heater. I pushed it up to *Full* and it still wasn't going to be enough. We punched through to the surface a minute later and I immediately forgot about the cold.

They'd taught me about Hell. But they hadn't mentioned the sky. A carpet of stars hung from horizon to horizon - a glittering jewel that had remained unseen for decades. I felt humbled in the face of such immensity. More than that, the open space filled me with such dread that I had to lower my eyes, unused as they are to looking at anything more than ten feet away.

I switched on the ore probe and let it run. I had nothing to do for hours now except hang there in the sky and try to ignore the stars that now seemed to be falling ever closer, threatening to wrap themselves around me, engulf me and drag me off to the black beyond.

I say this to give you some idea of my thought processes in those early hours. I know I am speaking of things you have been taught, things you have seen on the holovids for most of your lives. But nothing has prepared you for what is out there, what must be faced if we are to survive the time that is left to us. It is vast, it is empty, and it does not care.

It just does not care.

I had music turned up loud for most of the next few hours. It seemed to help, to stop the oppressive sky from beating me down into the ice that lay everywhere below me. I almost didn't hear the *beep* as the probe announced a finding.

I checked the co-ordinates and my heart sank. It was a four-hour flight away. I wasn't sure my mind could take so much open space, so much desolation. Then I remembered.

Ten short years. And twelve points short of my breeding merit.

I set my eyes on the brightest star, and told the probe to go.

I tried to let my mind wander, to think of happier times in the warren, of solid walls and enough light to keep the dark at bay permanently. But my eye kept drawing me back to that star, a bright pinpoint. At first I thought it might be one of the planets, before I remembered that, without a star to light them, they too had gone mostly dark. I realised that I was looking at Sol itself... or what was left of her after the dimming.

You've all seen the history vids, you all know of the great golden ball that some days seemed to fill the sky. And I know that some of you harbour thoughts that it's still up there, hanging above, and that we will walk underneath its heat again.

I wish I could show you that sad little point of light that is all that remains; I wish I could make you see just how far the dark has encroached since we went under. I flew over the desolation for hours. We know from our lessons that we went to ground where we hoped to be hottest. Iceland they used to call it, a place of hot springs and abundant thermal energy. Or so we thought. The dimming changed all of that; not quickly, but three hundred years without heat is a long time. And Iceland now lives up to its name.

There is no sea.

I'll repeat that, for it is something we have forgotten. We see the pictures, of waves crashing on sandy shores, and smiling people walking hand in hand under open sky. Never again. There is ice, pack ice, and rock. Nothing else.

I headed south and west. Again the history tells of cities, tall mighty monuments to our past. They are all gone. The ice has eaten everything. The history of mankind has gone cold. More than halfway into my journey I crossed what had been the Equator, what had been lush greenery. All gone. The whole planet has gone cold.

That was my thought and I saw nothing to make me change my mind.

Until I reached my destination.

And here I must take more care over my words. There are no histories that mention what I must tell, no pictures I can show you. Only what I have seen with my own eyes, and if I am to impress you with urgency, I must be clear in my intent.

The flyer told me I was somewhere in the South Pacific. It looked little different to the spot where I had come upside, but as we descended I saw that the ice here was less compacted. Several darker patches showed. As I got closer, I could see there were stretches of broken ice and slush. I started to think there might even be open water available. The probe beeped a proximity alert warning as the flyer hovered ten feet above an island of rock, black against the ice all around.

There was ore here, and a lot of it. The scan showed a seam, some one hundred feet deep in the rock. I quickly spotted that I would have to land and drill to get proof, for if the deposit was as large as it seemed to be, then more flyers would be needed to carry it back below to where it was needed.

I put the flyer down on the flattest spot I could find. I did not need to get out to supervise the drilling; the on-board bot handled that. But I could not come all this way to merely sit in a bubble. Even despite the glowering stars overhead, my curiosity won over my fear. I put on a helmet and ventured outside, aware even as I did so that I was probably the first human to walk above ground for three centuries.

I had to turn up the suit heater after just two steps. The helmet told me I had two hours power left, but I wasn't worried. I just wanted a short walk, just enough to be able to brag about it back in the warren.

The only sound was the steady grinding of drill on rock. My heads-up told me that the strata being drilled was sedimentary on top of schist, the drill currently penetrating rock that was over two hundred million years old, and going through a million years of sediment a second.

All of which was secondary to the fact that I had just found a cave.

The heads up told me that drilling would take another thirty minutes. And with the heater turned up full, I was cosy enough, despite the outside temperature of minus 65, a figure which meant nothing to me. Besides, I could always rationalise my decision to enter the cave mouth by telling myself I needed some respite from the lowering stars in the sky above.

I stepped into the darkness, and got a sudden fright when my helmet switched on a bright light to show me the way. I felt my heart pound in my ears and had to steady myself to quell the impulse to flee. But two more steps took me in to the cave proper, and I almost felt at home. The walls were smooth, some weathering process over the millennia was my assumption, and the light from the helmet was bright enough to light my way for twenty yards ahead. The cave floor sloped downwards, and as I proceeded the temperature rose. It was when it reached minus four that I was given pause for thought.

I might have discovered much more than just a source of ore. There was obviously heat here. And plenty of it.

I went in further.

Fifty yards in I had to turn off the suit heater. I also got the first indication that this was more than a simple cave. I found a number imprinted on the wall. It read:

SUB LEVEL 25.

The passageway was man made.

As you can imagine, my heart rate was elevated as I

went in further. We know from our history that we were not the only ones to go under; indeed we were communicating with some of the others for the best part of a century. But there has been no contact for more than two hundred years. The thought I might be close to meeting another human being made me descend even faster.

There was still no sound beyond the increasingly distant grind of the drill searching for ore. Neither was there any light beyond what my helmet provided. But it kept getting warmer. The heads-up told me there was only the thinnest of atmosphere beyond my visor, but it felt almost as if I walked a corridor in the warren.

I came to a junction and chose the right hand fork, heading deeper into the system.

I found the first corpse seconds later.

We are inured against death by our merit procedures. That, and the walk to the chamber when our time has come, means I have lived my whole life in the warren without seeing a dead person.

It is not pretty.

Pieces of dried skin hung in flaps from white bone. I was so appalled that it took me seconds to spot the important fact. The dead man had not been wearing a suit. He had died while there was still an atmosphere in the cave system.

Not being an expert, I had no way of telling how long ago that might have been, but judging by the decomposition of the clothing, I guessed that many years had passed.

I kept going, but I was no longer convinced I would meet anyone yet alive.

The corridor opened into a wider chamber, an eating area of sorts.

Bodies lay strewn everywhere, lying on mounds or pairs. Skeletal arms were wrapped around broken necks, skulls showed signs of having been bashed in against tabled and floor. They had all killed each other in a frenzied melee.

As I bent to inspect the closest, I saw the cause.

The darkness danced in their eye-sockets, a deeper shadow. It was full of stars where the sky had fallen in and got them.

The more I looked, the more I saw it; there in the shadow where a body hung over an overturned chair, there in the corner under the food processors, but mostly in the eyes, dancing and twinkling, mocking my horror.

I stumbled past more bodies than I could count, searching for a reason, an answer as to what had happened. The empty eyes followed me everywhere I went. There was a door opposite me, and I went through, hoping for some small escape from the terror.

I recognised where I was. The corridor structure almost exactly mirrored the structure of the warren here. Indeed, I began to fear for my sanity, thinking I had inadvertently returned home to find you all dead, all taken. There were no bodies in this part of the system, just long empty corridors, but that somehow only made matters worse.

I went deeper.

Although I was still safe inside the suit, the air seemed somehow thicker here, more oppressive; a faint trace of blue mist hanging in the air. If I were home, I knew I would be approaching the bionic plant. Despite the terrors of the eating area above, I was almost eager to visit the working parts of the site, as there may even be something salvageable there, something that would further prolong our own time here in the warren.

I descended a stairwell and walked out into their bionics plant.

Scores of pairs of eyes turned and looked at me, reflecting like twinkling stars in my helmet light.

They had once been human, that much was obvious. What was equally obvious was that they had not been so for some time. The skin was pale, almost translucent, their eyes large, like saucers in heads too small to hold them. They scrambled, on all fours, amid a pile of slurry that seemed thicker in places.

I gagged when I saw the first rib cage, the first thighbone.

They started to crawl towards me, piteously mewling like hungry kittens. Stars danced in their eyes.

I fled.

I will not tell of my flight from that place, save to say that I have deleted the co-ordinates from the systems. If you want the ore, you will have to send out another flyer.

But I would advise against it, for the darkness will come back with them. The sky will fall, and your eyes will fill with stars. The darkness will get inside, and it will consume you, as it did to those poor things in the bionics lab... as it has started to do to me.

It is vast, it is empty, and it does not care.

It just does not care.

EENY MEENY MINEY MI-GO

A MIDNIGHT EYE FILE

I wasn't even looking for a case that night. I had my favorite seat in a back booth at the Bon-Accord, and I was working my way along the taps of their new ale arrivals. I do some of my best work when I'm drunk... and some of my worst. The trick is to know which is which.

The night the trouble started I scarcely knew my arse from my elbow. My on-again, off-again, relationship with Liz was currently off, Doug was away at a conference on medieval middens somewhere in Germany and I had money to burn… or rather, to drink. I arrived in the pub at lunchtime, and didn't intend leaving until I had to. Davie at the bar kept anyone who looked like they wanted to talk away from me, and I drank, whisky chased down with beer and smoke. As my auld ma would say, I was *scunnered* and *crabbit* – no fit company for man or beast.

Beer helped. Beer always helps, if you have enough of it. I hadn't had enough of it yet, but I was working on it.

Some time in the late evening I became aware that there was a man I didn't know sitting across the table from me. He looked thin, to the point of emaciation, and intense, with a stare that told me he didn't like to be crossed. Everything about him from the set of his mouth to the cut of his suit looked too tight – *prissy*, to use another of my auld ma's words. He had a half-pint glass of beer in front of him, which was enough to tell me he wasn't a local. And he drank like an amateur, with small, careful sips, wiping the froth fastidiously from his lips each time. I already didn't like him, and he hadn't even spoken yet.

"Mr. Adams," he said. There was an accent there, for sure, but I couldn't quite place it. "I have a proposition for you. I have no problem with money, and I have plenty of it that could see its way into your wallet… if you are interested?"

It had taken me long enough, but I started to pay attention. I didn't stop drinking though, so perhaps my attentiveness wasn't all that it should have been. I only found that out later, of course. That first evening, the story had sounded plausible enough. I ordered another beer and let him talk.

"I need you to find me a man," he started.

"You're in the wrong bar for that," I said. "Although there's a few down in the Town Center..."

He didn't seem to mind my interruption, but went on as if I hadn't spoken.

"My son has gone missing," he said.

That told me a lot more than he thought. He didn't want the police involved, so something wasn't quite kosher... and he'd come looking for me in particular, so it was probably something funky. My reputation was getting around. It kept me in work, but I was starting to yearn for the days when the strangest thing I encountered was a cat in a coat or a husband in his wife's underwear.

I had missed a bit while ruminating and forced myself to pay attention.

"He was last seen outside the house last night," he said. "And I need him back, urgently. There is a certain time constraint in play here. If I do not have him back in forty-eight hours, then you don't get paid. If you are willing to undertake a promise to return him to me on time, I am willing to promise you five thousand pounds on delivery."

The rest was unspoken.

No delivery, no payment.

I'd read that much in his eyes. I don't usually work that way. Then again, I don't usually earn five grand for a couple of days work either.

"This isn't a kidnap case is it? Because that's the cops

domain, not mine,"

He shook his head.

"As far as I know, the boy has taken it into his head to go walkabout," he said. "And at the most inopportune moment imaginable. I merely want him back home, no questions asked. Now, do you want the five grand or not?"

I nodded, and put out a hand to be shaken. He looked at it as if it was a small naughty dog.

"I don't do physical contact," he said, primly.

"I'd guessed that already," I replied, but the innuendo went straight past him without stopping. "Tell me about the boy."

He took another small sip from his beer. I was near the bottom of mine, but he'd barely supped half an inch from his. I considered offering him another, but old age might get me before he got round to finishing it. Then, for the first time in our chat, he showed some animation as he talked of his son; his eyes lit with fervor, and something that looked too close to fanaticism for my liking.

"Andrew is my son and heir, what else do you need to know? He's five ten, twenty five, big built, and strong."

"Any distinguishing marks?"

He rolled up a sleeve and showed me a tattoo, a golden-yellow squiggle on the inside of his wrist; it could be anything, from a snake inside a circle, to a kid's impression of a squinting eye. But it would be recognizable enough.

"Andrew has one of these, exactly the same, in the same spot."

I got a tickle, the feeling I wasn't getting details that

I was going to need. That is the moment when I should have walked away. I can see that now, looking back on it. But a combination of booze and the thought of making an easy five grand had me bewitched. I just sat there as he described some peculiarities that would ensure I would recognize the boy when I found him.

I ordered another beer for myself, he passed me a business card, nodded briskly, and left.

Professor E. Penderton, and a Glasgow phone number. I turned it over. There was no address. I considered following him to check him out, but I couldn't trust myself to be discreet with so much booze in me. I concentrated instead on my beer.

At some point later I staggered home and fell asleep.

I didn't dream.

My first port of call in the morning was Old Joe downstairs in the newsagents. He passed me two packs of Marlboro Reds and I asked him about the Prof.

"I ken the man you mean," the old man said, swaying from side to side as he spoke as if balancing his weight equally on his feet. "Some kind of physicist I think; stars and planets, sky stuff like that."

"Sky stuff, eh? Sounds technical."

Joe laughed.

"You ken me, lad. Football, bookies and lines of credit I can handle, but hard sums is another matter. But if it is the man I'm thinking of, he's got a house out Balloch way, and one of yon big telescopes in his garden. I only ken because I ken a man who kens the man who built the observatory for him."

Joe knows a lot of men who know a lot of other men,

but he couldn't help me with Penderton's son. He smiled as I had to move aside to let a customer approach the counter.

"Sorry, Derek; I just ken about the sky stuff."

Over a smoke and a coffee I spent some time at my laptop upstairs. There weren't many Andrew Pendertons in Glasgow, and only two with current phone numbers. When I dialed the first I got a retired Govan brickie who was very chatty, and more than a bit sad; I liked him, but I liked the idea of five grand better, so didn't rise to the bait of his attempts to get into a conversation. The second number rang out to voicemail but I didn’t leave a message; I prefer legwork when I can get it, it brings me into closer contact with places I can buy a drink. My reverse look-up app gave me an address in the West End only a mile or so from my office, it wasn't raining, and I was developing a thirst, so I headed out and up Hyndland Road in search of adventure. Admittedly, there's normally not a great deal of that to be found at the top of Partickhill Avenue, and that morning was no exception.

The streets were quiet, it being both a work and school day. I was heading for number 23, and the only other person on the road was an elderly lady, out on her doorstep throwing lumps of bread at a flock of squalling pigeons, seagulls and crows as if she was trying to hit them with it.

"Give one a skelp for me," I shouted as I walked past.

"Go fuck yourself," was her measured response, and one that set the tone for much of what followed that day.

Number 23 sat back a bit from the street, almost hidden in shadows cast by the taller red sandstone buildings around it. It was a typical example of an older Glasgow tenement, spruced up just enough to be rented out to students more worried about cost than comfort. There wasn't a front door; an open, tile-lined close led into a cold drafty hallway. They had one of those old things by the side where you could press a button to check if the person was in, but it hung halfway off the wall, loose wires showing. I'd have had better luck in standing in the street and shouting, but I wasn't in the mood for a grand entrance.

I went into the hall and started climbing the dark staircase up to flat six in search of Andrew Penderton, who had used the address when registering his phone some four months previously. The place reminded me far too closely of my own student digs. They were spent in a flat much like this, less than two miles from the spot; too hot in summer, too cold in winter, too damp the rest of the year, and always smelling faintly of stale beer, fried food and pish. It carried far too many memories for one staircase. Nobody answered at my knock on the door of number six, and I wasn't all that disappointed, for I could imagine what might lie on the other side – more memories I didn't need to have surfacing. I was about to turn away and head for the first beer of the day when the door of number five opened at my back.

"I don't what you're selling, mister, but there's naebody here as will buy it."

I fixed on my best smile before turning to face her; a wizened old woman, bent with age and arthritis, with a face like old leather and eyes as blue and clear as sapphires.

"You're not selling anything, are you?" she said, looking me up and down and immediately gauging the cost of my suit and finding it wanting. "What are you? Polis? They should pay you enough to get a better jacket."

"No, not Polis," I said. "I'm looking for the Penderton boy – his faither is worried for him."

"That'll be a first," the old lady said, cackled like a crone, and did something disgusting with her top set of false teeth, sliding them in and out as if they were an extra, hard, tongue.

"You know the boy?"

"I know them all, son. I'm like their auld grannie; they all come to me with their problems, but mainly I think they just like my biscuits. Would you like a cup of tea? There's nobody in across there; I think they're all down at the Uni or over in The Rock playing pool."

"The Rock? They drink in there?"

"They spend most of there time in there; I don't know when they get time to study. Tea?"

Just another lonely soul, desperate for a voice, any voice, to fill the empty spaces in front of the fireplace. Normally I'd have gone in – old Scottish women always have great biscuits and fancies, it's a law I think. But the five grand wasn't going to wait.

"I'll take a rain-check," I said. "But if I don't find the lad by tea time I'll be back."

"You'll not find him here after dark either," she replied as she backed away, leaving me one last look at her falsers sliding in and out. "They're off down to yon big old church in Duke Street tonight for a party."

The Rock bar on Hyndland Road has changed hands

more often than an inveterate wanker over the years. Every so often a new owner upgrades the décor in the hope of getting a better class of clientele. But no matter what the management do, the same locals and each new generation of students just keep coming, meeting in the bar and over the tables in a shared love of beer, card games and pool. The older locals make enough money off the young students' naivete, and the students go away happy thinking they've got an authentic slice of Glasgow life. Things hadn't changed since I'd been one of those students, more years ago now than I care to remember.

Now I was one of the locals. Gerry at the bar was pouring my pint while I was still walking across the floor towards him.

"A wee Goldie to go with that?" he asked, and motioned at the whisky optics.

"Nah, I'm working," I replied. "Save me one for later."

"Working? In here?"

I nodded toward the pool table where four male students were currently playing.

"You wouldn't happen to know if one of them is Andrew or Andy Penderton?"

Gerry followed my gaze.

"There is an Andy with that crowd usually – well built lad, posh accent..."

"... tattoo on the inside of his arm?" I asked. "A squiggly yellow golden thing?"

Gerry nodded.

"That's his pals at the table now, but I haven't seen him for a few days. Is he in trouble?"

"His auld man's looking for him, and is willing to pay

good money to get him home. So far, that's all I know. I'll go and talk to this lot, but if you see him, you've got my number... there's fifty quid in it for you if I find him before tomorrow night."

I took my beer over to the pool table.

I didn't introduce myself, just watched them play, then put some money on the edge of the table, indicating that I'd play the winner of the current game in play, double or nothing on my stake.

It was like taking candy from babies.

After an hour I was thirty quid up, I'd bought them all a few drinks and, softly-softly, got them round to the subject of their flat, and their absent friend.

"Aye, his old man's been on the phones this past twenty-four hours," one of them, a lanky streak of pish called Stevie said. "Is Andy in trouble?"

I shrugged.

"Not with me. His father asked me to check in on him, that's all."

Stevie had drunk more than a few beers, and that, and youthful bravado, shone through strong.

"Tell the old man what Andy told him yesterday," he said. "Tell him Andy says Fuck Off."

"They don't get on?"

Stevie's voice dropped low so that only we round the table could here.

"It's weird shit, man," he said. "Andy says his father has gone gaga. Fucking UFOs and aliens and all that crap. He wants Andy to help him with some kind of experiment, but Andy's having none of it."

I pressed, not too hard, for more, but there wasn't

much more to be had, beyond the fact that I knew where my target was going to be later; at a party in the big converted church in Duke Street with the rest of them.

Now that I knew where my man was going to be I was in no mood for pounding the streets; not when there was beer on hand. I spent the next few hours playing pool, cribbage and dominoes, eating stale cheese rolls and shooting the breeze with old pals, and new.

I thought I'd got all I could out of Penderton's flatmates, but I was proved wrong later that afternoon; Stevie, the thin lanky one, joined me in the Beer Garden for a smoke, and lowered his voice, as if someone might be listening in.

"That stuff about the UFOs... you'll not tell anybody I mentioned it, will you?"

I laughed.

"What's the matter? You're not worried about the Men in Black are you."

"No, not them... something else. We've all heard it, up on the roof of the house. There's a good reason Andy's staying away."

"Stop havering, lad. Just tell me what you're on about here."

"That's just it. We don't know. We think Andy does, but he buggered off as soon as we all started hearing it."

"Hearing what?" I said, nearly shouting. "Get to the bloody point, son."

"Chittering," he said softly. "Lots of chittering; like a million insects at once, all of them angry."

I was smart enough to leave The Rock before I got to the stage that I wouldn't leave until they threw me out. I went back to the apartment that I call my office, spruced up, had some coffee and a few smokes, then headed straight back out again.

Party time.

The last time I'd been down Duke Street to the converted church, it had been called Goth One and catering to the black-for-every-occasion crowd. I hoped this wasn't going to like that night; things had got hairy.

The queue snaked back for a hundred yards or so through the old graveyard and onto the road. This lot were more of your normal city-center party crowd; a mixture of students, wide-boys, lassies with more bare flesh than sense and predators, their eyes gleaming at the thought of the drugs they could sell, the flesh they could peddle; just another night out in the big city.

The church itself was lit up like a Disney fairy castle, its promises worth as little. Floodlights swirled and bounced off the old steeple and crenellated walkways and there was a distant throb of what might be music or might be a vibration from the Underground; it was difficult to tell them apart. When I got to the head of the line the bouncer looked me up and down.

"You're thirty years too late," he said. "Come back tomorrow, it'll be bingo night and the women will be more your age."

I gave him a twenty, and all my trouble went away as quickly as the note vanished into his pocket. As soon as I got inside I wanted to return and ask for my money back.

The place was, as they say in Glasgow, heaving. A couple of hundred damp bodies bounced in time to a rhythm that was all bass and nothing much else, lights flashed just off the beat, too bright, and there was a stench in the air of sweat, beer and desperation.

I'd always been too old for this crap.

I walked the perimeter, studying faces, looking for a tattoo. I saw skinny Stevie, pissed as a fart, strutting his funky stuff in front of some lassies who couldn't quite conceal their boredom, but there was no sign of Andrew Penderton, and the crowd was getting more dense by the second. Soon it looked like one huge organism, seething and roiling as if in the throes of birth. Or maybe it was just getting ready to take a shit; either way, I didn't feel like staying around to watch.

I went back out onto the steps. The queue had all made their way inside, and the bouncer leaned at the side of the door. I joined him in a smoke, and showed him another twenty.

"I'm looking for a lad," I said. "Stocky built, well spoken, and a tattoo, here..." I motioned on the inside of my wrist."

"A squiggly yellow thing? Aye, I know the lad."

I waved the twenty in his face.

"And? Tonight?"

He nodded and took the note.

"Last I saw of him he said he was taking a lassie upstairs to see the view from the top of the steeple. I sometimes let them up there."

If they slip you a note.

I didn't have to say it; we both knew the score.

"Right through the back, the door on your left will see you to the stairwell. Be careful. It's dark, cold and slippery."

He was right on all three points.

I found the door easily enough, right where he said it would be, then had to grope in the dark for three steps before I caught a glimmer of light above me, just enough to show me the way up. After a couple of flights of narrow stone steps the sound of the party faded, although I still felt the vibration in the soles of my feet, channeled through the stone directly into my bones; it was all I could manage not to climb in time to the beat.

The light above grew brighter; at first I thought I was looking at the swirling floodlights above the steeple, but this light was an internal one, pouring down from a chamber that was now only one flight of stairs overhead.

Somebody was speaking. I didn't want to walk in unannounced on the lad if he had a girl up here, so I stepped up close enough to listen in, but far enough back in the stairwell that I wouldn't be seen.

I needn't have bothered.

A youth, I guessed it must be my quarry Penderton, spoke some words I couldn't quite make out. Whatever answered, it wasn't a girl. It was a chittering.

Lots of chittering; like a million insects at once, all of them angry.

The youth's voice grew angry in reply, shouting now, a yell with more than a hint of fear in it.

"No," he shouted, and I heard a scuffle, and another yell from the lad, this time of pain. That was my cue to rescue any chance I might have of getting my five grand. I stepped into the room.

The lad was wrestling – at first I thought dancing

– with a heavy set, short figure wearing a long, floor-length leather duster coat and a wide brimmed hat pulled down over his face. The flickering lights I'd noticed on the stairwell came from a globe high in the ceiling that seemed to hang there, without any visible signs of anything holding it up. But I didn't have time to give it any attention; the heavy-set figure seemed intent on dragging the lad, and my five grand, away.

"I will not come," the lad shouted.

I heard chittering again. Skinny Stevie had indeed described it almost perfectly...and it wasn't a sound any human throat could have made. I tried to keep a tremor out of my voice as I spoke.

"You heard the lad," I said. "He's staying here. And you'd best get going if you don't want any trouble."

The stocky chap turned towards me. His face was in deep shadow under the brim of the hat, and I couldn't see any eyes, but once again I got the feeling I wasn't looking at anything human.

I stepped forward, close enough to make a grab for the lad if I needed to.

"There's no need for any of this," I said, keeping my voice calm, even as I aimed a kick for the assailant's groin. I didn't meet flesh; I didn't meet anything I expected. Beneath the coat everything was soft, squishy, and my kick brought a sour, sickly smell into the room that threatened to make me lose my earlier beers. It had the desired effect though; he let go of the lad, and retreated across the chamber from us.

I pressed my advantage, stepping in again for another blow, and would have got one in too, if the globe of light above us had not winked out, casting us into momentary darkness. I heard a flutter, accompanied by more chittering, and then a flap as of huge wings, which reminded me more than anything of the old lady feeding the birds earlier. One of the floodlights outside swirled round towards where we stood and I stared into Andy Penderton's frightened face.

He stood on the other side of the chamber from me, and there was a leather coat and a wide brimmed hat lying on the floor at his feet.

The lad was still shaking when I offered him a smoke back down in the quiet graveyard outside the church. He kept looking up towards the steeple, as if expecting another attack. It was only after he accepted a cigarette that he looked at me.

"Who the fuck are you?"

"I'm the fucker that just saved your life, but don't rush to thank me all at once."

"No, I mean it. What were you doing up there?"

"I was about to ask you the same question."

He laughed.

"We could do this dance for a while you know? I'm guessing from the suit that you're not here for the party. You're from him, aren't you? The old man sent you."

"Aye. He's worried about you."

"Is he fuck. He's worried what'll happen tomorrow night if I'm not there, that's all."

"And what will happen?"

Penderton got a look in his eye I knew only too well; he was getting ready to run. I put a hand on his arm.

"Look, son, I'm here to help."

"Not if you're working for my father you're not. How much is he paying you?"

"Five grand."

He laughed.

"Is that all. I'll give you ten if you let me go, right now."

"I can't do that. But I can get you somewhere safe, and I can listen to persuasion. I think you've got a story, and I need to hear it. Deal?"

We shook hands on it over another smoke, and I took him to the safest place I knew.

He almost took fright and ran as the taxi dropped us off outside *The Twa Dugs*.

"Are you daft, man?" he said. "This is too close to home. My flat's just up the hill there."

"Aye, I know," I replied, ushering him toward the door. "It has two advantages; nobody will think you that stupid, and, as I said, it's the safest place in the city. Trust me."

George was in his usual spot behind the bar, and gave me a raised eyebrow when he saw I had the lad in tow.

"Trouble?"

"A wee bit," I replied.

"Polis trouble?"

"Not that I know of. This is trouble of the unusual kind."

George knew me well enough not to press the matter in public.

"Do you want the back room or the cellar?"

I knew what he was asking; the back room was for polite conversation, whereas the cellar was where questions were asked rather more forcibly, away from anybody who might hear the screams.

"The back room," I said. "And best get the lad here a pint of heavy. He's got a story to tell, and he'll need lubricating."

"I'll get one for all of us, on the house," George said.

The back room of *The Twa Dugs* is no more than ten feet square, with peeling wallpaper, three battered armchairs, a coffee table and an ancient two-bar electric fire, but that wasn't what made it the safest place in the city; George's reputation saw to that.

George was the bar's owner, but he was also a provider of favors to some of the richest and most influential men in the country. Everyone from police to politicians, reporters to sportsmen, came under his domain, and he had fingers in great many pies. All of which meant that the rest of the city's criminal element knew better than to cross him and George was left alone to maintain a growing empire. We were safer here than if we were in the cells below Maryhill police station.

Penderton was still skittish, but he settled after the first beer went down and we all had a smoke.

"You're not going to believe me," he said when I asked again for his story. George replied for me.

"Laddie, unless you're another fucking werewolf, I'm willing to bet your story isn't even going to be the strangest one Derek has brought to the bar."

The lad's eyes went wide at that, but I didn't have time to get into old stories of my own; there were too many to tell in one night anyway.

"Your old man had me believe there was a time element involved here?" I asked, trying to get him started.

"Aye. The gathering is tomorrow night. But to explain why that's important, I have to go back a year or two to when it all started."

He spoke, and we listened over beer and smoke.

"I was still at school when father started to get a bit strange. It wasn't long after he had the observatory built in the garden; he spent most of his nights out there, either watching the skies or poring over old star charts. I caught a glimpse of them once; ancient dusty things drawn on vellum, faded and worn. But when I asked father what relevance they had for modern astronomy, he never answered, merely studied the charts with even more concentration.

"Groups of people came and went at all hours, well to do men in expensive cars who never smiled. I rarely saw father at all, for by then I was banned from the observatory. I could only look out from my bedroom at night and wonder at the causes of the dancing aurora of lights, or the source of the harsh, distant chanting in a language I could not fathom.

"One day last summer, just before I moved here to go to Uni, he made me a very peculiar offer; he told me that he would fully fund my course, and all my expenses, if I would get a tattoo done to his specifications. I thought he was mad of course, but you know how strapped for cash you can get here, so I went along to that wee parlor off Renfield Street, and the old man sat bedside me while I had this done."

He rolled up his sleeve and I saw it was indeed the exact replica of the one his father had shown me; a yellow squiggle in a circle.

"Is it meant to represent anything?" George asked.

The lad smiled grimly, and accepted another smoke from me.

"I'll get to that soon enough. It's at the center of the whole thing though, I can tell you that much."

Once he got his cigarette lit, he went back to his story.

"For a wee while I was too busy with my life to worry about his, but when I went home or Christmas I saw a change in him, and it wasn't for the better. He was more or less living in the observatory, sleeping by day and spending all night at the scope. I quickly ascertained that he was only watching one area of the sky, but I couldn't figure out why until he told me.

"'It will be closest in late spring,' he said. 'That is when they will come again, and we must be ready to meet them. They have much to teach us, if we allow the to take us with them.'

"It took me a while after that to figure out what he meant. It's a long story that I won't go into detail here, but the gist of it is that my father is a member of a UFO cult. They believe that aliens from Pluto – Yuggoth as they call it – are coming here looking for the best and brightest to take them away; save them from the coming catastrophes, if you believe that kind of crap. My father certainly believes – they all do, all of the folks who carry this same tattoo. You see, it's a representation of the alien's home, and it's like an invitation for them to take us away. My father believes they are coming tomorrow. He's organized a party and some kind of ritual welcome for them at the house in Balloch. That's the reason he sent you after me; he's going to go with them...and he wants me along for the ride."

George laughed, and punched me lightly on the shoulder.

"Easiest money you'll ever make, Derek. Take the lad home and get your cash before the faither comes to his senses."

His laugh faltered when he saw the look on my face.

"The problem is, it's not a load of old bollocks, is it?" I asked Penderton. "These things are real, and I met one earlier, in the steeple."

The lad went pale and nodded.

"I was drawn up there, as if hypnotized. If you hadn't come along when you did, I might be gone with them already."

For once George was stumped for something to say. I can't say as I blamed him.

"You won't make me go back to him," the lad said, and he suddenly seemed much younger than before, a terrified boy rather than a young man. "You won't let them have me?"

"Don't worry, lad," I said. "I'm not in the habit of turning metaphorical damsels in distress over to big bad wolves, even for five grand."

"That's good," the boy said, and managed a thin smile, "for I don't have ten to give you anyway. But what do we do?"

George answered for me again.

"You'll stay right here until after tomorrow night, if you've got any sense. We can see what's what after that."

Penderton looked at me.

"If you say it's the right thing to do?"

I nodded.

"I'll stay with you, and George will make sure nobody disturbs us... him and I have played this game before. You're safe here. Get comfortable; you're going to be sleeping in that chair."

"In that case, can I have another couple of pints and a packet of fags?"

He was a lad after my own heart. He liked his beer, he liked to smoke, and he played a strong game of chess, as we found out over the next few hours. He also liked to talk. I learned of a mother died young, of a lad brought up in a world of astronomy, physics and mathematics who disappointed his old man utterly by choosing to prefer English Literature as a career path. Just by talking to him I could tell he was a strong willed youth, and he showed no sign of being overly shaken by his earlier experience, not beyond what I'd expect anyway. I certainly liked him a lot more than I liked his father.

I also learned a bit more about the purported 'Space Cult' but to my ears it was the usual Californian influenced wishful thinking bollocks that had been so popular in the Sixties. If anyone was daft enough to think that wee green men were going to take them away to a better place, I was happy to leave them in their delusion.

There was only the one thing bothering me though; I'd definitely encountered something out of the ordinary early in the steeple; I just wasn't sure yet what it had been.

We chatted, drank, ate snacks from behind the bar

and played chess through until the early hours of the morning. I looked up after considering a move to see that Penderton had dozed off, sitting upright in the chair. I left him to it, and went through to the bar, where George was clearing up and washing the glasses from the night before. There was no one else in the bar.

"It's a good story, I'll give him that," George said to me. "But is it really worth five grand? All it will take is a phone call, his faither will be here to take him off your hands, and you'll have enough cash to pay your bar tab."

"Steady on," I said, smiling. "I'm not sure I'm ready for that kind of commitment."

George looked me in the eye.

"Seriously, Derek. You don't need to look after every lost puppy, you know?"

I nodded.

"But when the alternative is watching somebody giving them a kicking, I don't really have a choice. There was something after that boy earlier, and it wasn't looking for a kiss, a cuddle and polite conversation."

After George finished washing the glasses he broke out the good stuff and we shared a couple of glasses of Speyside malt over a smoke, talking about nothing of consequence. I wasn't aware that I'd been waiting for something, but when it came I knew I had been expecting it all night. I heard it just after I stubbed out a smoke.

It was a chittering.

Lots of chittering; like a million insects at once, all of them angry.

I was closer to the door, so I headed out and into the corridor first, with George right at my back as we got to the room. We were too late.

It looked like the same thing I'd seen earlier, and either it had retrieved its disguise, or there had been a sale of long leather dusters and wide brimmed hats. It stood behind the chair in which the Penderton lad still slept, unaware of the danger looming over him.

The chittering was louder now, bringing with it a vibration that tingled in my gut, growing stronger still as the noise level increased. It felt like a million insects, burrowing and cavorting in frenzy in me and through me. I screamed, but there was no sound but the chittering, and they kept burrowing, eating away at my soft innards and starting on my bones until there was little of anything left of me. I'd been hollowed out, nothing but empty space, darkness, and twinkling stars.

Some time later I woke sitting upright in an armchair. George slept in the chair opposite.

There was no sign of Andrew Penderton.

When I woke George and we went through to the bar, a watery sunlight greeted us in the front window. Whatever had happened, it had put us out for hours; plenty of time for whoever, or whatever, had done it to make away with the lad.

"What the fuck happened there?" George asked. "That bastard thing was in my head, eating my brain."

"Aye, that's what I felt too. Some kind of Jedi mind fuck is my guess. And I'm also guessing I'm not the only one working for the boy's father. I was just bait in the trap."

"So what now?" George asked.

"Now I'm going to Balloch to make sure no harm

comes to the lad," I said. "And if any fucking wee green man gets in my way, it'll get a boot up its arse."

George didn't offer to come with me, but he did offer me backup, in the form of the sawn-off shotgun he kept under the bar 'for close encounters.'

"I've never been keen on shooters, you know that," I said, "I prefer to use my good looks and charm to keep me out of bother."

George laughed.

"Aye. How's that working out for you?"

He tried again to offer me some help.

"At least take a couple of the lads with you, just in case."

I shook my head.

"It's broad daylight. Your boys would stand out like a sore thumb in Balloch. Besides, daytime is good for me in this case. Have you ever heard of UFO abduction happening in daylight? No, these things prefer the dark; it gives them a chance to show off their expensive fairy lights. I'll be fine. I'll just walk in and have it out with the old man; there'll be no trouble. I could blow him over."

By the time I reached Balloch it was already mid-morning and I wasn't quite so sure of myself as I'd been earlier.

The taxi dropped me off at the gate of a large Victorian era house in a patch of woodland to the north west of Balloch, bordering on the shore of Loch Lomond. It was a secluded spot, made more so by overgrown luxurious rhododendron bushes and tall chestnut trees scattered in profusion through extensive grounds. I made no pretence of secrecy; I was a PI on a case, heading to meet a client, so I had my excuses ready to get them in early should anybody ask.

Nobody did.

I had a game to play here, cat and mouse to find out who knew what, and how much. I hadn't decided on an opening gambit until the door opened and the elder Penderton greeted me on the step.

"Mr. Adams, good to see you. Do you have any news on Andrew?"

I'd been watching his eyes; he'd be shite at poker, for he couldn't tell a lie without looking at my left shoulder; Jim Jeffries has the exact same tell, and I've taken him to the cleaners frequently due to it.

So, it's going to be like that is it?

I was going to push for answers, but not too quickly; if the lad was here somewhere, held against his will, I wasn't going to be any help to him blowing the case open too early. So when the older man stood aside to let me enter, I shook his hand, and stepped over the threshold."

"I found your lad last night," I replied as he showed me into a well-appointed library in the old, grand style, all oak shelves, mahogany fittings and whisky decanters. He didn't have one himself, but poured me enough for the two of us, but I was to only sip at it as he motioned me to an armchair.

"The boy is safe?" he asked, and again his gaze settled on my left shoulder.

"Aye. And he told me all about your little cult here," I replied. "Before I hand him over, I need assurances that he's not going to be harmed."

Penderton smiled.

"Assurances is it? Well, you've got nothing to fear on that score. A great future waits for him; for all of us. A future among the stars, not tied to this dying planet with its petty squabbles, a future of intellect and study where all are equal under scientific exploration."

"Well, that all sounds Utopian enough to me," I replied. "So why is the lad so scared of the prospect?"

"You know that already, Mr. Adams," Penderton said. "And we can stop beating about the bush here. You know the lad is already home; but we're glad you came for him, for you are a witness that cannot be allowed to tell his story. The world is not yet ready for such revelation."

"So what are you going to do? Abduct me and stick a probe up my arse?"

"Yes to the first, but as for the second, we have something far more interesting in mind; you shall join us among the stars and we will all go together into the bright new future."

I sensed it before I heard it, the chittering again, coming closer. I pulled the handkerchief out of my suit pocket and ripped it in two, intending to force the cotton into makeshift earplugs, but I was much too late. The noise got louder, a vibration taking hold in my jaw, in my skull and all down my spine, and again I had the sensation of being hollowed out to my core as I fell down into a black place full of swirling nebulae and stars.

I woke to a blinding light in my eyes and a distant hum that was all too reminiscent of the one I had fled my senses to leave behind. It was several seconds before my sight adjusted and I was able to take in my surroundings, and when I did so I half-thought I was still unconscious, still in the throes of a fevered dream.

I was securely tied, hands behind me, roped to a tall metal column—a support stanchion, and one of many that ran around the edge of a tall circular observatory dominated by a large central telescope. A dome of glass and chrome arced high overhead; in style and substance the structure was more like a Victorian greenhouse than a modern building, but it was a most impressive feat of architecture nonetheless.

The interior space was full of shining metal and sparkling crystal, a bewildering array of objects—obviously mechanical—whose purpose I could not even begin to discern. High above, the whole observatory was lit by two large shining globes of white light that seemed to hover without support a yard or so below the dome of the ceiling. A vibration came from the metal and glass contraptions—lights pulsed and static cracked, sending a short burst of blue sparks running up one wall before dissipating in the dome.

The younger Penderton was tied to the next stanchion in sequence to my right. He smiled thinly when he saw I was awake.

"Welcome to the future, Derek," he said, and motioned with his head that I should look to my left. Someone stood there with his back to me, bent over a long table, obviously intent on some task. It took me a second to realize it was not even remotely human. I finally got a good look at what had been under the long coat and wide-brimmed hat.

It was the size of a grown man, but looked more like a

hideous shrimp. The body was segmented and chitinous like that of a crustacean, but this was no marine creature —it had membranous wings. The wings were currently tucked tightly against its back, giving it a hunched appearance, and judging by the size of the hunch, they would be adequate to lift its weight into powered flight— and more than large enough to look almost like a leather coat when pulled around the body.

There were no arms or hands to speak of; I counted four pairs of limbs. The pair the thing used as legs—I use the word loosely here—were more stout and thicker than the rest, each being tipped with three horny claws extended to balance its weight at the front while a segmented tail completed the tripod behind it.

The other appendages looked more flexible and nimble, and as I watched, the thing leaned forward and delicately picked up a tool from the table. It turned slightly as it did so, and for the first time I got a good look at its face—or rather lack of one. Instead of features, there was only a mound of ridged flesh, pale and greasy, like a mushroom towards the end of its cycle. A multitude of thin snake-like appendages wafted around its head, and I took these to be the equivalent of sensory organs, although quite how they might function,

It was preparing for surgery. The older Penderton lay on the table beneath it, naked as the day he was born, his head completely shaved in readiness for what was to come. He was fully conscious. He saw me looking, and smiled.

"Now you will see the glory that is waiting," he said. "I will show you the way to a future without fear."

I have no idea what form of alien science accomplished what happened next – it was like some kind of flash magician's trick to my eyes. Within seconds, and with only a few deft strokes of a tool that seemed to cut and cauterize in the same movement, the back of Penderton's skull was laid open. The creature took up another tool and made a long slit down the length of the backbone, but the man was still fully conscious throughout, and showed no sign of pain or even discomfort.

"Goodbye, son" he said, and smiled. "I shall see you on the other side."

The crustacean thing moved aside to fetch a tall cylindrical jar of glass and silver. Penderton winked at me; the creature leaned forward and, using three limbs at once, tugged in a single sharp movement, swiftly lifting and turning to drop the detached brain and spinal column as a bloody mess into the jar, where it floated in a thick fluid, as if suspended there. The body jerked, just once, and then slumped—stone dead without the controlling influence of his senses.

There was more to come: the creature lifted the jar —which must have weighed several stone at least—and carried it to a long metal wall. With a wave of a limb, a door slid silently open to reveal a shelf running around the outside wall of the observatory, stacked tightly with more of the tall jars, each of which had a brain and spinal column floating inside like some mutant jellyfish. I guessed this was what remained of the other members of the cult.

Within seconds of Penderton's brain being added to the line, a misty haze of dancing light filled the space before us. It seemed to come from everywhere yet nowhere, accompanied by a distant hum. The light and color coalesced and thickened, hanging into a flattened oval. The surface dulled to a flat gray, and an image formed—a head, out of focus at first and then sharpening to clarity. Penderton's smiling face looked straight at us.

He spoke, echoing his earlier words.

"Welcome to the future."

The face turned to look at Andrew.

"Pure intellect, unburdened by the day-to-day need for sustenance, untainted by the filth and grime of modern living—no need for conflict or strife—an end to war. Join me, lad—the Mi-Go can take us away, show us the stars; we can travel out and meet our destinies."

The Mi-Go turned back towards us, heading for the Pemberton lad.

"Remember what I did in the steeple," I said, "if you get a chance."

The lad winked at me, then turned back to address his father.

"Now that I see what has become of you, I'm ready, father," he said.

The old man took that as acceptance, as he was meant to. The Mi-go, using talons as sharp as knives, cut the boy's bonds and led him toward the bench for surgery. Andrew dropped his left shoulder, rolled away and, still turning, put all his weight into a kick that caught the Mi-Go in what should be its groin area.

The result was immediate—the creature fell in a heap to the floor; and it was within reach of my feet.

I stomped down, hard, my right foot sinking deep into its head. It came apart in a splash of gore. The thing's limbs thrashed wildly. Flesh sloughed and ran, hissing and bubbling in a noxious mess. The snake-like tentacles whipped and curled in frenzy before going still only seconds later. There was a last, moist, gurgle; then the top third of the thing fell apart in wet ooze. The tang of strong vinegar scorched my nasal passages.

"No!" the older Penderton shouted. "What have you done?"

"I've chosen freedom," the lad shouted back. "Freedom from you, and the tyranny of your kind. You can take your pure science and shove it up your arse."

He was definitely a lad after my own heart.

He went to where the Mi-Go had placed his father's brain and lifted the jar off the shelf before dashing it to the floor. Broken glass and spinal fluid lay among the spilled fluids, mingled which the still bubbling remains of the Mi-Go.

The whole structure of the observatory rattled. The globes of light dropped like stones and smashed into glittering fragments of glass and crystal, leaving us in a dim gloom. Old Penderton's image wavered, a shocked, silent, scream the last thing to be seen before it broke up into wispy shadows and was gone.

Glass shattered overhead as a vibration shook the whole building.

"Time to go lad. Get me out of here."

More glass cracked overhead, shards tumbling to crash around us. The coils and tubes hummed and throbbed, and a vibration ran through the observatory, setting the whole place shaking, building to a climax.

"This place is going to blow any second."

Andrew managed, with some fumbling, to get my bonds freed and, arms across each other's shoulders, heads down and crouching, we headed for the door.

We only just made it, although even so, the force of the blast when it came was enough to knock us flying into a patch of bare earth.

I spat out mud and turned to see the observatory collapse in on itself, the telescope itself the last to go as it tumbled down in a roaring cloud of dust and buried Penderton's remains under a mound of iron and glass.

Young Andrew was still trying to get up, still focused on the remains of the observatory, so he did not see it. Indeed at first I wasn't sure I had either—it was merely a darker shadow against the night sky, standing on top of the remains of the telescope. Then wings opened out, obscuring the stars behind them. It launched itself off the cliff and into the sky.

Something chittered in the distance, a million insects, fleeing the scene.

The last I saw of it was as it crossed the face of the moon, still heading higher, the wings unfurled and soaring.

MORE LOVECRAFTIAN FICTION

THE PLASM

INTO THE BLACK

I discovered the writing of H P Lovecraft back in the very early Seventies in secondhand British paperback editions.

I came to him, not looking for horror, but for Science Fiction as that was where my prime interest lay back then. I believe the first story I read was THE DUNWICH HORROR in one of those paperback editions.

That was enough for me to seek out the rest, and I still remember a first reading of AT THE MOUNTAINS OF MADNESS while sitting on the back steps of our house on a hot summer's day. From there I quickly found Derleth, Clark Ashton Smith and the whole Weird Tales alumni and they in turn led me up to more relatively modern times via Bloch, Matheson and Ramsey Campbell.

It was only natural that I should turn to some Lovecraftian conceits in my own writing, and in recent years I've found there's a wide variety of markets willing to share this wee corner of my obsession, from the likes of Dark Regions Press, The Lovecraft Ezine, Chaosium, Golden Goblin Press and a variety of anthologies and magazines.

My list of Lovecraft-inspired works grows apace.

HOME FROM THE SEA

Get the Willam Meikle newsletter and get a free ebook starter library

https:www.williammeikle.com/newsletter.html

Made in the USA
Coppell, TX
20 October 2026

93449777R00041